Trainspotting

#1 Lust For Life

Iggy Pop

Words & Music by David Bowie & Iggy Pop

Moderate Rock (♪♪ played as ♪³♪)

(𝄋) Here comes _ John-ny Yen _

I'm worth a mil-lion in

a-gain with the liq-uor and drugs and the flesh ma-chine. _

priz-es with my tor-ture film, drive a G. T.O., _____ wear a

He's gon-na do an-oth-er strip tease. Hey man, where'd you get _ that

un-i-form all on a gov-er-ment loan. I'm worth a mil-lion _ in

Trainspotting

International Music Publications Limited
Southend Road, Woodford Green, Essex IG8 8HN, England

Wise Publications
London / New York / Sydney / Paris / Copenhagen / Madrid

Distributors:

Music Sales Limited
8/9 Frith Street, London W1V 5TZ, England.
Music Sales Pty Limited
120 Rothschild Avenue, Rosebery, NSW 2018, Australia.

Order No. AM938180
ISBN 0-7119-5858-0
Visit the Internet Music Shop at
http://www.musicsales.co.uk

International Music Publications Limited
Southend Road, Woodford Green, Essex IG8 8HN, England.
International Music Publications Limited
25 Rue D'Hauteville, 75010 Paris, France.
International Music Publications Gmbh, Germany
Marstallstrasse 8, D-80539 Munchen.

Order Ref. 4188A
ISBN 1-85909-379-5

Music arranged by Roger Day.
Music processed by Paul Ewers Music Design.
Book design by Michael Bell Design.

Printed in the United Kingdom by
Caligraving, Thetford, Norfolk.

ear be - fore, _ 'cause of a lust for life, 'cause a

To Coda ⊕

1

no chord

lust for life.

2

I got a lust for life, _

got a lust for life.

Oh, a

#2 Trainspotting

Primal Scream

Words & Music by Bobby Gillespie, Robert Young,
Martin Duffy & Andrew Innes

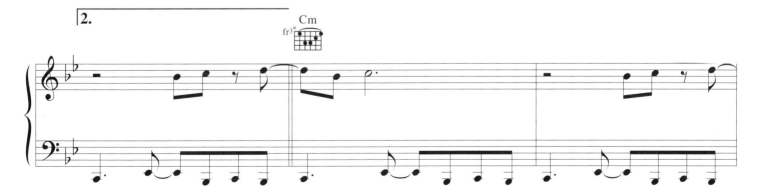

9

#3 Deep Blue Day

Brian Eno

By Brian Eno, Daniel Lanois & Roger Eno

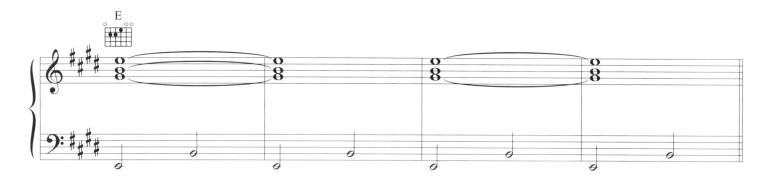

Repeat to fade

#4 | Atomic

Sleeper

Words & Music by Deborah Harry & Jimmy Destri

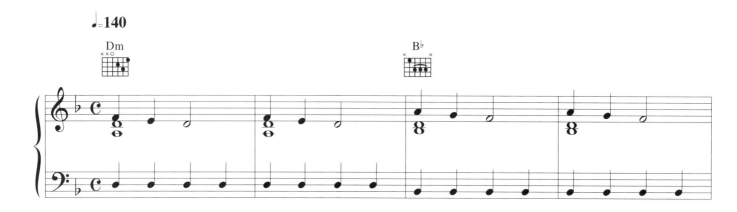

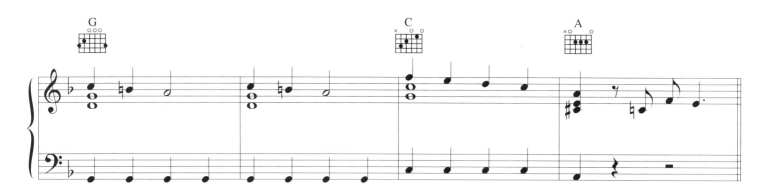

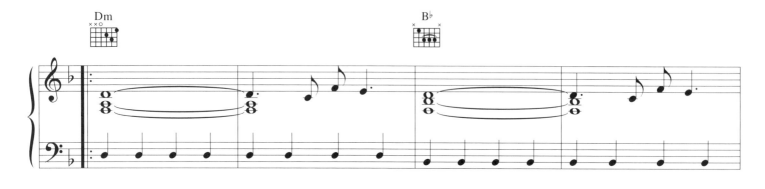

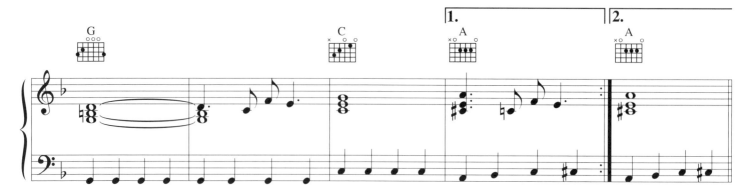

Oh   oh oh____ make me to - night,_____ to -

night_____ make it right._____

(1.) Oh   oh oh____ make me to - night,_____ to -
(2.) Oh   oh oh____ make it mag - ni - fi - cent_____ to -

night,   to - night.____
night,   right.____

Oh your hair is beau - ti - ful,

oh_____ to - night._____ A - to - mic.

To -

#5 | Temptation

New Order

Words & Music by Peter Hook, Stephen Morris,
Bernard Sumner & Gillian Gilbert

Ooh _____ ooh _____ ooh _____

_____ ooh _____ ooh _____ ooh _____ ooh _____

_____ ooh _____ ooh _____ ooh _____ ooh _____

1. Hea - ven, a gate - way of hope.—
(Verses 2 & 3 see block lyric)

just like a feel-ing I need— it's no— joke— and though it hurts me to treat— you this way you treat my words I ne-ver heard— too hard to say.—

Verse 2:
Each way I turn I know I'll always try
To break this circle that's been placed around me
From time to time I find I've lost some need
And what's emerging to myself I do believe.

Verse 3:
Oh you've got green eyes, oh you've got blue eyes, oh you've got grey eyes
Oh you've got green eyes, oh you've got blue eyes, oh you've got grey eyes
And I've never seen anyone quite like you before
And I've never met anyone quite like you before.

#6 Nightclubbing

Iggy Pop

Words & Music by David Bowie & Iggy Pop

Moderately slow shuffle (♫ played as ♩♪)

Night-club-ing,   we're night-club-bing,   oh, is-n't it wild?___
night-club-ing,   bright white club-bing.   Oh, is-n't it wild?___

31

#7 | Sing

Blur

Words & Music by Damon Albarn, Graham Coxon,
Alex James & Dave Rowntree

#8 Mile End

Pulp

Words by Jarvis Cocker. Music by Pulp

1. We did-n't have no-where to live, we did-n't have
(*Verses 2 & 3 see block lyric*)

no-where to go, till some-one said, I

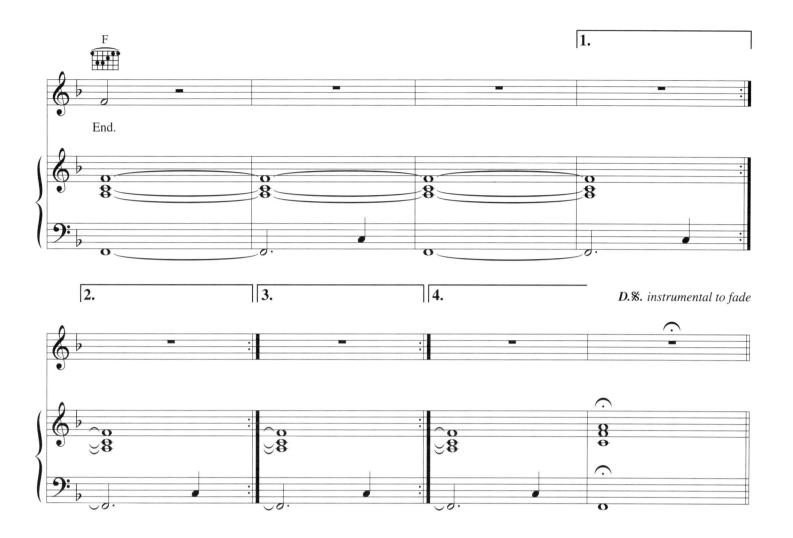

Verse 2:
And now we're living in the sky
I never thought I'd live so high
Just like heaven
If it didn't look like hell.
The lift is always full of piss
The fifth floor landing smells of fish
And it's come Friday
Every single other day.

Then a load of kids come out tonight
They kick a ball and have a fight
And maybe shoot somebody
If they lose at pool.

Verse 3:
Nobody wants to be your friend
'Cause you're not from round here
As if that was
Something to be proud about
Look there's the king of the Isle of Dogs
Feels up children in the bog
Stand by one of the playing fields
Someone sets a car on fire.

I guess you have to go right down
Before you understand just how
How low, how low, a human being
Can go.

#9 Perfect Day

Lou Reed

♩.= 58 Words & Music by Lou Reed

Just a per-fect day __ drink san-gri-a in the park, __ and then la-ter when it gets dark, we go home.

Just a per-fect day, __ feed a-ni-mals in the zoo, __

Verse 2:
Just a perfect day
Problems all left alone
Weekenders on our own,
It's such fun.
Just a perfect day
You made me forget myself
I thought I was someone else,
Someone good.

#10 For What You Dream Of

Bedrock featuring KYO

Words & Music by John Digweed, Nick Muir &
Carol Leeming

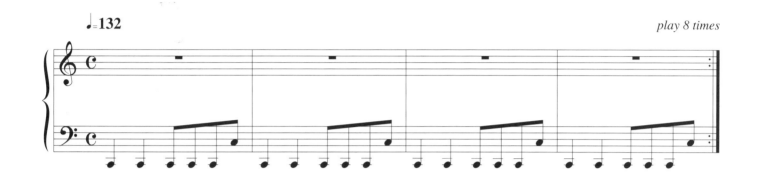

For what you dream of. For what you dream of. For what you dream of. For

1, 2. what you dream of. **3.** For what you dream of. When the tak-ing and the giv-ing starts to

get too much, let the mu-sic hit you with its heal-ing touch.___ Life's

tree___ is as tall___ as its ma - ny branch - es,

but not all___ God's child - ren___ have the same___ chan - ces.

instrumental
break ad lib.

46

Repeat to fade

Let your-self___ be be-neath your___ mind___
(See block lyric)

don't you know___ that you can have a se-cond chan-ces, re-mem-ber the fu-ture and

ne-ver look back,___ lis-ten to the spi-rit while your bo-dy dan-ces.

You're losing your mind, but that's okay,
You're lost in the cool smoke of, lost in the cool smoke of
Hell of ages, you're caught up in love,
You walk the fire for what you dream of.

Repeat ad lib. to fade

#11

2:1

Elastica

Words & Music by Donna Matthews

1. Keep-ing a brave face in cir-cum-stan-ces is im-pos-si-ble, can-not
(Verse 2 see block lyric)

des - cribe so ma - ny de - ci - sions, it's im - pos - si - ble to know— which is— the pro - per or - der, the best po - si - tion to be in. Take ad - van - tage or so it seems, the way— it goes.

Verse 2:
Tragic, laid down on your side
Too easy, you know that
You know you're soaking wet
You talk too much, it's not necessary.

Before the ice melts
I just want to say this packet's yours
Don't ask for more
'Cause somewhere along the line I've forgotten already.

Sandman comes two to one
In the dark, dark reflections
In my bed, in my head
Again.

Sandman goes two in tow
Wet and dumb, three's the number
Coming round
Coming down again.

#12 | A Final Hit

Leftfield

Words & Music by Neil Barnes & Paul Daley

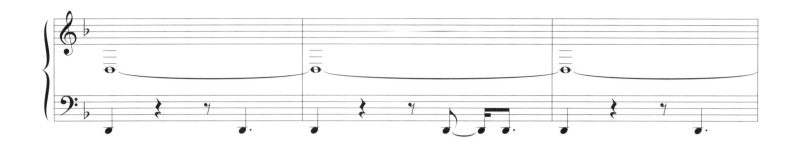

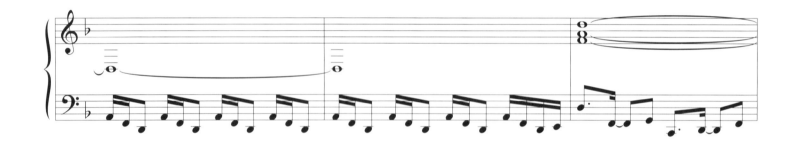

Repeat to fade

#13 Closet Romantic

Damon Albarn

Words & Music by Damon Albarn

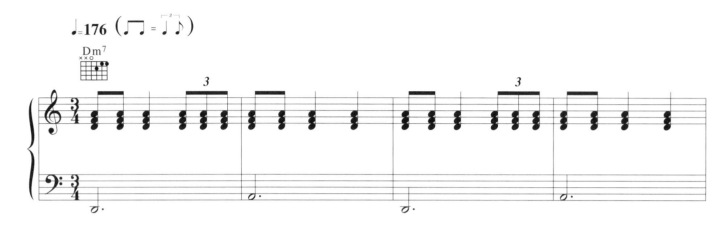

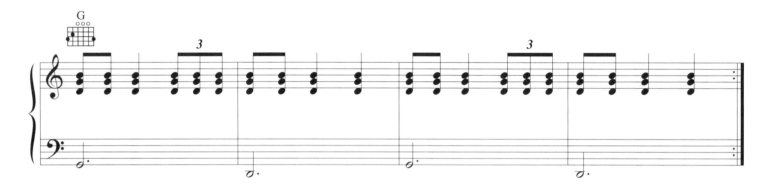

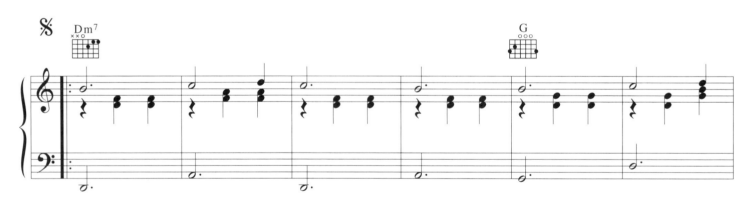

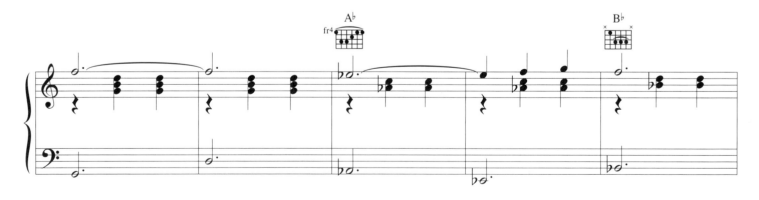

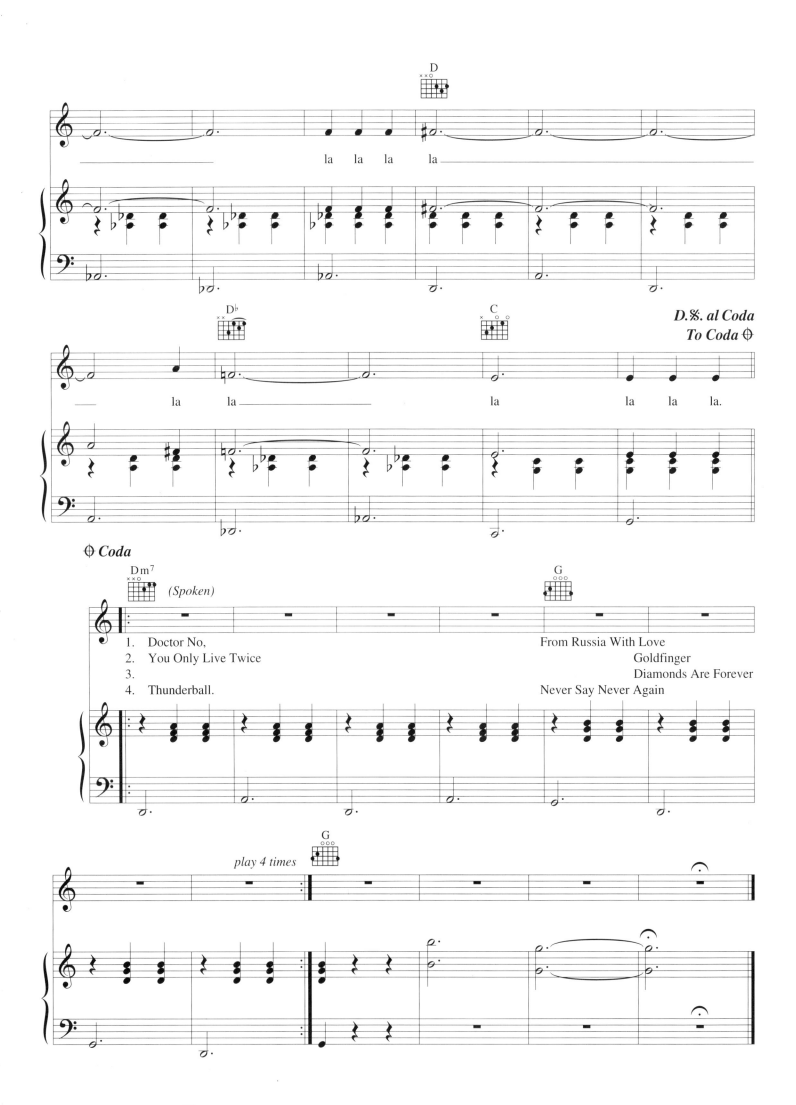

la la la la

D.%. al Coda
To Coda ⊕

la la la la la.

⊕ Coda

(Spoken)

1. Doctor No,
2. You Only Live Twice
3.
4. Thunderball.

From Russia With Love
Goldfinger
Diamonds Are Forever
Never Say Never Again

play 4 times